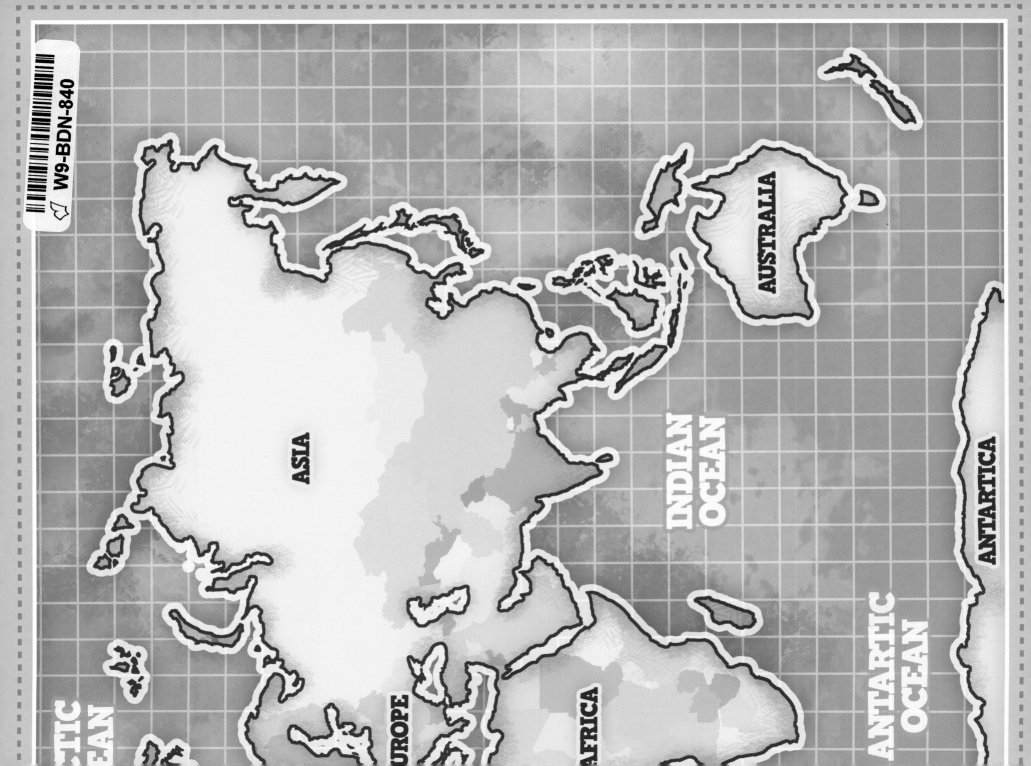

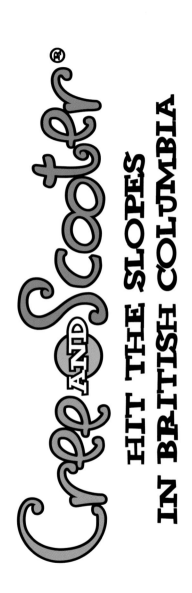

Cree and Scooter®

HIT THE SLOPES
IN BRITISH COLUMBIA

The Adventures of Cree and Scooter: A Global Series

Softcover ISBN: 978-1-936449-17-0

Hardcover ISBN: 978-1-936449-02-6

Library of Congress Control Number:

2010940039

This book was printed in the United States of America.

Publisher's Cataloging-in-Publication Data

Sutton-Brown, Tammy.
  Cree and Scooter hit the slopes in British Columbia /
Tammy Sutton-Brown ; illustrated by Joel Cruzada.
    p. cm.
  ISBN: 978-1-936449-02-6
  1. British Columbia–Juvenile fiction. 2. Canada–
Social life and customs–Juvenile fiction. I. Cruzada,
Joel, ill. II. Title.

PZ7.S9688 Cr 2011
[Fic]–dc22
2010940039

To order additional copies
of this book, contact:

Hugo House Publishers, LTD.
Englewood, Colorado
(303) 762-1469 or (877) 700-0616
www.HugoHousePublishers.com

Hugo House

Cree and Scooter®

HIT THE SLOPES IN BRITISH COLUMBIA

The Adventures of Cree and Scooter: A Global Series

Country: Canada

Continent: North America

By Tammy Sutton-Brown

Visit us at www.CreeandScooter.com

For

my parents, Jean and Monroe,
who instilled in me the value of reading.

♥ A Letter from Cree ♥

Before I met Scooter, I did not like naptime. Now my dreams are lots of fun because Scooter comes to life whenever I go to sleep. He takes me places all around the world while I dream. I like Scooter.

He is smart. He knows all about other countries, their languages, and foods. He understands how people live.

Boy am I glad that Scooter loves adventures like me. Everyone sees Scooter as a stuffed toy, but to me, he's more than that. Scooter is my best friend. I am learning so much as we travel to different countries. Get ready to come along with Scooter and me as we explore and show you the world!

Cree

Cree loved stuffed animals, especially ones
that fit in her backpack.
"Here you go Cree," Omar said, handing
his sister a stuffed toy.

"He is very special. His name is Scooter, and he is a chameleon. He is really cool. You should take him on vacation. I am sure he will enjoy Canada with us."

Cree dashed out of Omar's room, hugging Scooter tightly.

Thanks Omar!!!!

As Cree packed her favorite things into her backpack, she began to wonder what Canada was all about. All of a sudden, she heard her favorite song on the TV.

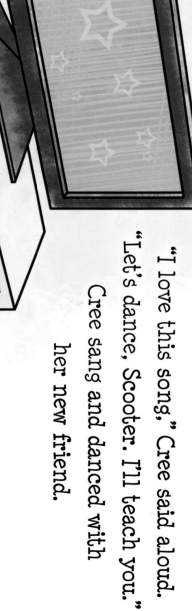

"I love this song," Cree said aloud. "Let's dance, Scooter. I'll teach you." Cree sang and danced with her new friend.

"I boogie to the left like a leaf in the wind.
I boogie to the right while trying to blend in.
I jump up and down changing colors in the light.
I crawl on the ground trying to stay out of sight."

"Honey, I have a surprise for you," Cree's mom said as she entered the room. Cree's eyes sparkled as her mom held up a shiny piece of jewelry.

"Wow! A bracelet," Cree exclaimed.

"Yes dear, it is a charm bracelet. I had a bracelet like this when I was a little girl. I decorated it with charms that I collected from all of the places I visited. I thought it might be nice for you to collect charms on our trip to Canada tomorrow."

"Thanks Mommy, I love it," Cree replied.

Cree's dad came into her room to say goodnight. As Cree's eyes began to close, her mom softly whispered...

"As we close our eyes,
in every dream, there's a new surprise.
Open your mind, use your imagination,
for tomorrow you will explore
a new destination."

With Scooter in her arm,
Cree fell asleep
and started to dream…

Suddenly, Cree and Scooter were seated in an airplane, ready to take off.

"Cree," Scooter was saying, "fasten your seatbelt, just like you do in the car."

"Scooo...ter," Cree said. "You're talking! How is that possible?"

"Special things happen when we dream."

"Wow!" Cree exclaimed with glee. "This is going to be the best plane ride ever!"

"Scooter, please tell me more about chameleons," Cree begged her friend.

"Chameleons are part of the reptilian family. Some people call us lizards. We do some special things. I can move my eyes one at a time. Can you move your eyes one at a time?" Scooter asked.

Cree tried to move her eyes one at a time, but they kept moving together.

Scooter laughed and said, "I didn't think so. Humans can only move their eyes together. Another special thing about us is that we change colors," Scooter continued.

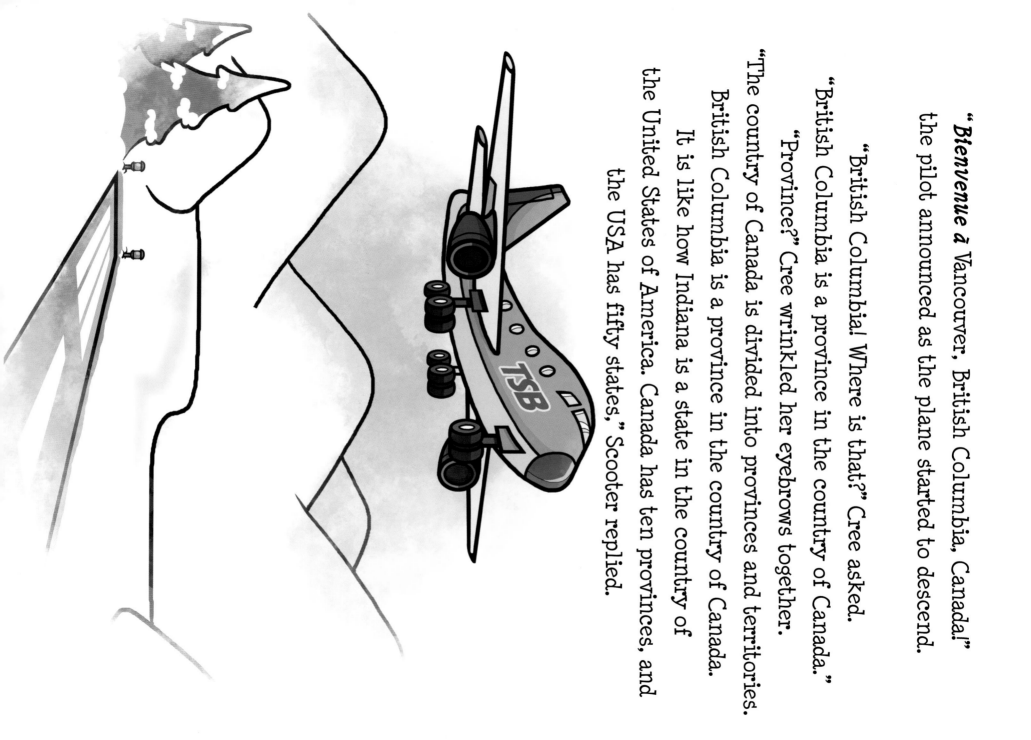

"*Bienvenue à* Vancouver, British Columbia, Canada!" the pilot announced as the plane started to descend.

"British Columbia! Where is that?" Cree asked.

"British Columbia is a province in the country of Canada."

"Province?" Cree wrinkled her eyebrows together.

"The country of Canada is divided into provinces and territories. British Columbia is a province in the country of Canada.

It is like how Indiana is a state in the country of the United States of America. Canada has ten provinces, and the USA has fifty states," Scooter replied.

"Scooter, what else did the pilot say?"

"He said *bienvenue*. That means 'welcome' in French. There are parts of Canada where both English and French are spoken."

"How did you know that Scooter? Do you speak French?" Cree asked.

"*Oui*, I speak French. I also speak many other languages," Scooter responded.

"That's really cool, Scooter."

"What's *Oui*?" Cree asked with a giggle.

"*Oui* means 'yes' in French."

"I like that. *Oui*," Cree said.

She liked to test out new words.

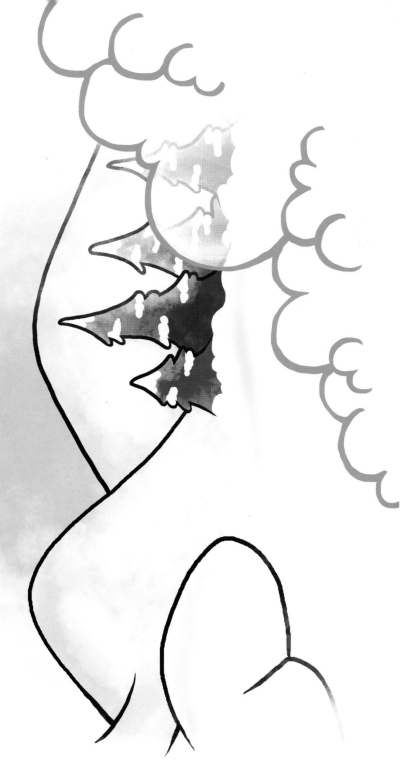

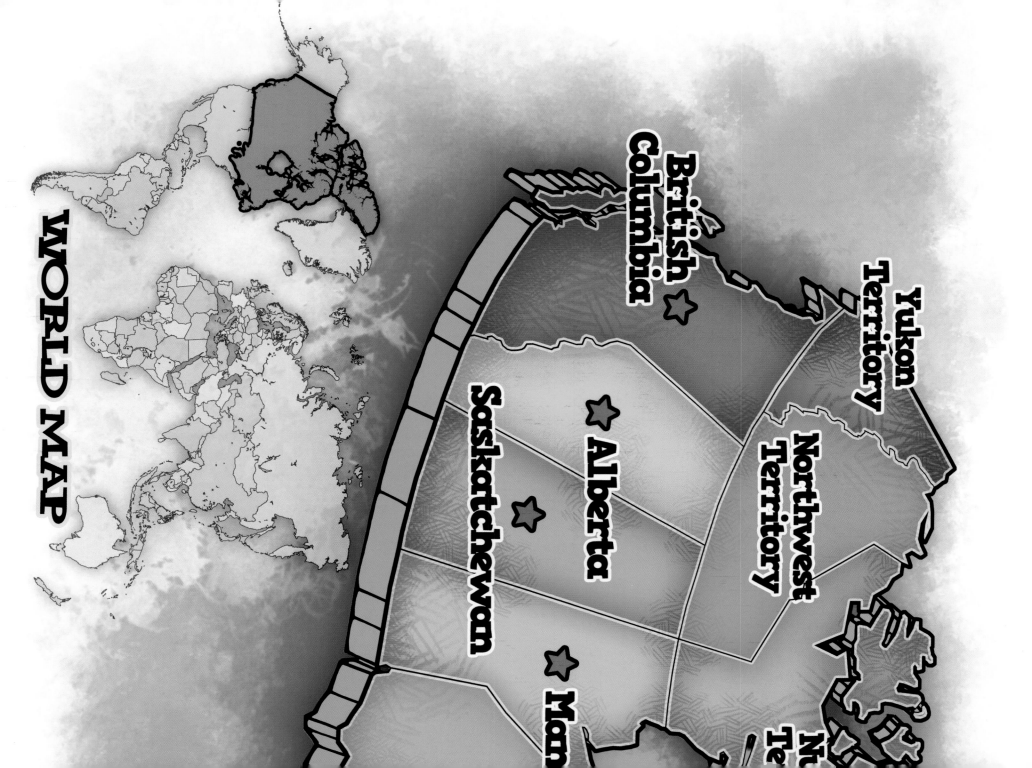

WORLD MAP

British Columbia ⭐

Yukon Territory

Northwest Territory

Alberta ⭐

Saskatchewan ⭐

Man...

N... T...

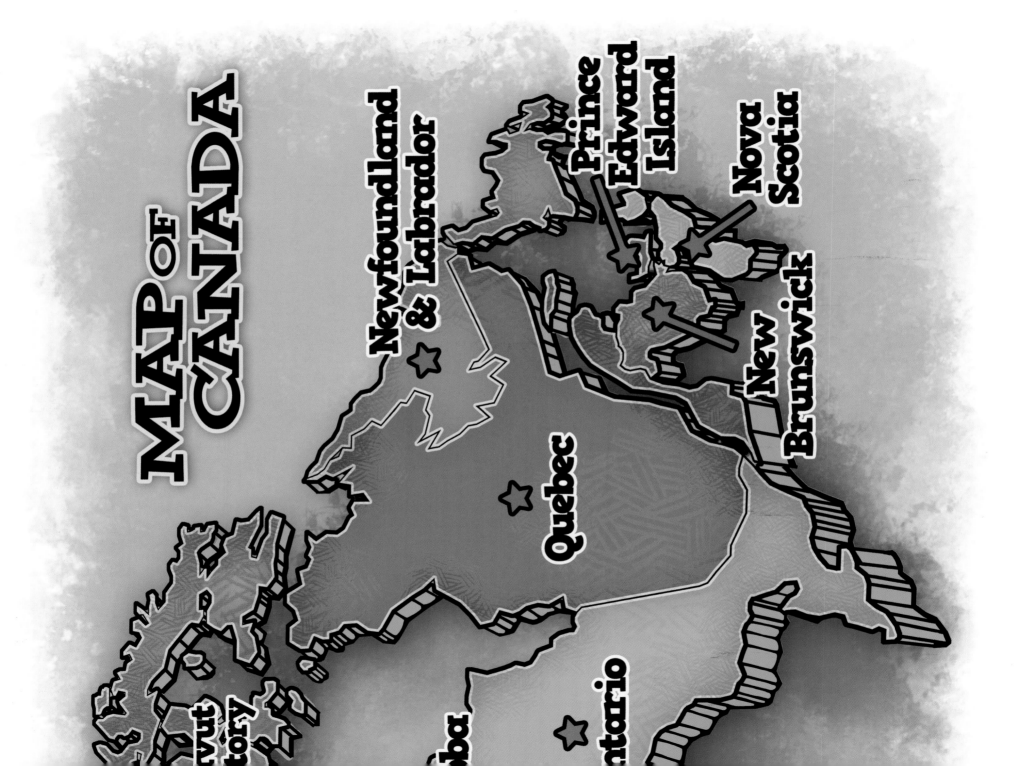

MAP OF CANADA

Newfoundland & Labrador

Prince Edward Island

Nova Scotia

New Brunswick

Quebec

Ontario

Manitoba

Nunavut

Territory

"Teach me more, Scooter!"

"D'accord. D'accord," Scooter said.

"What!" Cree said as she put her
hands on her hips.

"D'accord means 'okay' in French."

"Oh okay, I like that."

"D'accord," she repeated. She tried not to giggle,
but the word felt funny to say.

Cree realized she enjoyed learning a new language.

As they waited for the plane to land,
Cree saw Scooter pull something
from her backpack.

"What's that, Scooter?" Cree questioned.

"It is my passport," Scooter replied, while showing her the small, dark-blue book.

"What's it for?" Cree asked.

"We must have a passport to show the authorities in Canada so that we can be allowed to visit the country. I have one for you right here," Scooter said as he handed Cree her passport.

"Thanks, Scooter. You sure think of everything. I didn't know that I needed a passport to visit Canada."

The plane landed moments later. Scooter hopped into Cree's backpack, and Cree walked out of the airport and into the cold air. To Cree's amazement, a purple Scooter popped out of her backpack.

"Scooter, you're a different color!" Cree gasped.

"Yes, I am. Whenever I am cold, I turn purple. My blue color will come back once I get used to the weather," Scooter explained.

"Let's take a taxi to Whistler," Scooter said as he shivered.

"They had the 2010 Winter Olympics there, right?" Cree asked.

"*Oui*," Scooter replied. "Whistler is a resort town in Vancouver, Canada with world-class skiing."

"Scooter, where is Vancouver?"

Scooter removed Cree's handheld computer from her backpack.

He pulled up the map of Canada on the screen.

"Look, it's right there," Scooter said. "It is in the province of British Columbia, which is right above the state of Washington."

"Okay, now I understand," Cree responded.

"Want to know something really neat about Canada, Cree? Canada is the second largest country in the world!"

"Wow! You know a lot about Canada," Cree said.

Cree looked at the towering mountains covered in white snow.

"Scooter, there is snow all around! It doesn't snow where we live. It looks like there are giant marshmallows everywhere."

The taxi finally arrived at the ski lodge at Whistler Mountain. Cree pointed to the largest mountain that rose above the town.

"Scooter, is that Whistler Mountain?"

"Yes, it is!"

Scooter pulled Cree's binoculars from her backpack and focused on the mountain.

"Look, you can see people skiing!"

"That looks like fun!
I want to ski," Cree shouted.

"Do you know how to ski, Scooter?" Cree asked in amazement.

"*Out*," Scooter nodded.

"Can you teach me?" Cree asked.

"We should find a ski instructor to teach you how to ski safely."

As they entered the resort's souvenir shop, Cree looked over at the glass case filled with souvenir charms.

While Scooter arranged for her skiing lesson, Cree purchased her first charm.

"I can't wait to show Mommy my new charm.
It is so cool. It is of a girl skiing.
That's going to be me," Cree proudly stated.

With her new charm firmly secured on her bracelet, Cree joined Scooter and their ski instructor, Mr. Todd, as they boarded the ski lift. Cree waved to the skiers below. She felt like a champion skier as they rode the ski lift to the top.

"Mr. Todd, I am glad to have you teach Cree how to ski. After all, I can't teach her everything!" Scooter said jokingly.

Cree and Mr. Todd laughed.

Mr. Todd showed Cree how to bend her knees
and let the long, flat skis glide over the snow.
He also showed her how to turn her skis
to the side to slow down.

"Are you ready to give it a try?" Mr. Todd asked Cree.

"Yes," Cree replied.

With Mr. Todd's help, Cree moved slowly down the slope. Scooter skied beside Cree, swishing back and forth.

"Whoa!" Cree shouted as she sped down the mountain on her skis.

"Phew! Skiing is scary," Cree gasped.

"It is, but you did well. You made it down the mountain on your first try without falling. You should be proud. You're a great student," Mr. Todd told Cree.

Cree broke out in a wide grin.

"Scooter, how do you say 'thank you' in French?"

"*Merci,*" replied Scooter.

"*Merci,* Mr. Todd," Cree said with a giggle.

"Do you speak French, Mr. Todd?" Cree asked.

"*Oui*, just a little," Mr. Todd said. "My family's culture is Chinese, but I was born here. British Columbia has the largest Asian population in Canada. As you travel, you will see there are a lot of different cultures to celebrate in Canada."

"I'm sure Scooter will teach me all about that," Cree said as she looked at Scooter who winked back at her.

"**Merci** for teaching me how to ski, Mr. Todd."

"No problem," said Mr. Todd. "**Au revoir**, Cree. **Au revoir**, Scooter," he continued, smiling as he skied away.

"Scooter, I think he was saying 'goodbye.'

Am I right?" Cree asked.

"**Oui**, Cree, that was good. You used his gesture to figure out what he was saying," complimented Scooter.

"**Merci** Scooter," Cree replied as she turned to look at him.

"Scooter, I want to ski down the slope again.

Will you come with me?"

"Sure," agreed Scooter. "Let's go."

Cree and Scooter made their way back to the top of the mountain. As they came off the ski lift, they spotted something in the distance.

"Look over there," Scooter said pointing.

"It looks like a bear," Cree stated.

"I have never seen a white bear before."

"It's called a 'spirit bear,' Cree. These bears are special. They are in the black bear family but have white fur and are found in the central and north coast of British Columbia."

"They are so cute. I wonder if I would be allowed to have one as a pet," Cree said, laughing loudly as they started skiing down the slope.

Cree enjoyed seeing the snow-covered trees along the way.

Suddenly, Scooter crossed in front of Cree.

Startled, Cree lost her balance and plowed into a high snow bank.

Scooter! Scooter! Scooter!

"Scooter, you knocked me down," Cree yelled.

Scooter could not answer. He was buried
head-first in a bank of snow.

"Scooter, where are you?"
Cree cried out. She was scared.

Cree started to dig frantically in the snow because she knew that chameleons cannot survive in the cold.

It didn't take long for Cree to uncover Scooter. He was bright yellow like the sun.

"Scooter, are you hurt?"

Scooter shook his head and moved his eyes one at a time to make sure he was all right.

"No, I'm okay now, but I was really scared. I turn yellow when I'm scared," Scooter explained.

Cree turned to Scooter,

"I don't know what I would have done if I didn't find you." Cree almost started to cry.

"You're my best friend, Scooter!"

"It's okay, Cree. I'm sorry I got in your way. I skied too fast and lost control."

"I guess we need to practice more," Cree said. "You know what, Scooter? That was really fun, even when you knocked me over!"

They both laughed.

"Yeah," Scooter agreed. "Skiing is fun. Let's go down the slopes again! I'll race you!"

As Scooter ran off, his color started changing back to blue.

"Scooter," Cree called after him. "You're turning blue again. Now I know why you change colors. You do it when you're scared or cold."

"Or when I'm being chased," Scooter teased.

Together, they ran across Whistler Mountain.

"Cree, honey, it's time to wake up," Cree's mother said.

She pulled the covers back, and looked puzzled as she noticed the new charm on Cree's bracelet.

"Mommy!" Cree exclaimed.

"What is it dear? Did you sleep well?"

"*Out.* Oh Mommy, I had the best dream ever.
Scooter and I had so much fun!"

With a curious look on her face, Cree's mom
wondered where she learned the word '*Out.*'

As Cree's mother walked out of the bedroom,
Cree jumped excitedly out of bed with Scooter in hand
as she danced the chameleon dance.

"I boogie to the left like a leaf in the wind,
I boogie to the right while trying to blend in,
I jump up and down changing colors in the light,
I crawl on the ground trying to stay out of sight."

Cree was definitely excited about her trip to Canada!

Meet Tammy Sutton-Brown

WNBA veteran and two-time All Star, Tammy Sutton-Brown was born and raised in Ontario, Canada. However, she has spent more time living abroad than in her home town.

Tammy believes that exposure to various cultures, languages, traditions, and values enhance the quality of one's life. This philosophy has motivated Tammy to travel extensively. She has visited more than forty countries across five continents.

Tammy's commitment to social initiatives is exemplified in the Tammy Sutton-Brown Foundation, Inc. (TSBFoundation), which was founded in 2009. This non-profit organization is committed to the empowerment of women and children.

To support this cause, some of the proceeds from the Creep and Scooter® adventure book series will be donated to the TSBFoundation.

Cree and Scooter® GLOSSARY

ENGLISH		FRENCH		PRONUNCIATION
yes	→	oui	→	wee
thank you	→	merci	→	mair-see
welcome	→	bienvenue	→	be-en-ven-u
goodbye	→	au revoir	→	oh rer-vwahr
okay	→	d'accord	→	dah kor

For more fun and exploration

Visit us at www.CreeandScooter.com

Cree AND Scooter®

Thanks for joining Cree and Scooter on their trip to the province of British Columbia in the country of Canada on the continent of North America. Cree and Scooter enjoyed having you take part in their adventure. You were with them for the whole ride!

Keep your passport safe, because you are going to need it for the next trip. Start packing your bags and get ready to join them on their next destination to the country of China on the continent of Asia.

In the meanwhile practice your French and continue the fun, in the Cree and Scooter Activity Zone.

See you next time!

Tammy

BONUS FUN!

Attention Kids: We wanted to give you something extra special and fun to show you our appreciation for buying our first book. Enjoy!

NAVIGATOR FUN!

Help Cree & Scooter find their way around the world by drawing a line from the list of continents and oceans below, to the correct area on the map.

CONTINENTS

- North America
- Australia
- South America
- Antartica
- Africa
- Europe
- Asia

OCEANS

- Antartic
- Atlantic
- Indian
- Pacific
- Arctic

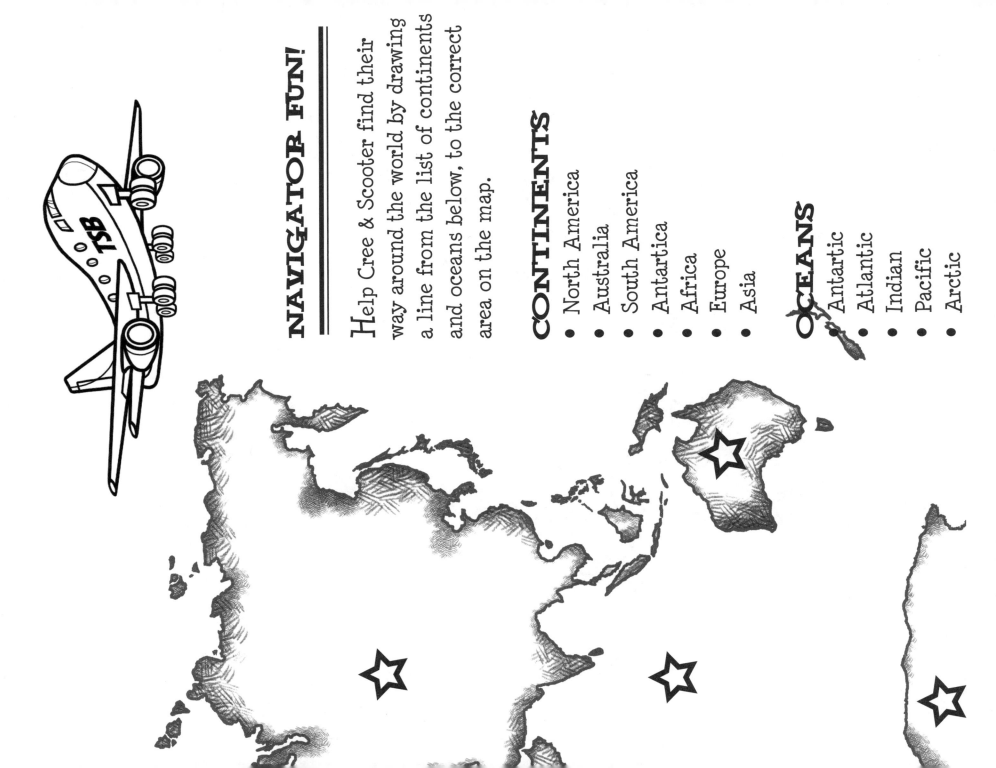

Cree and Scooter are excited for their trip.

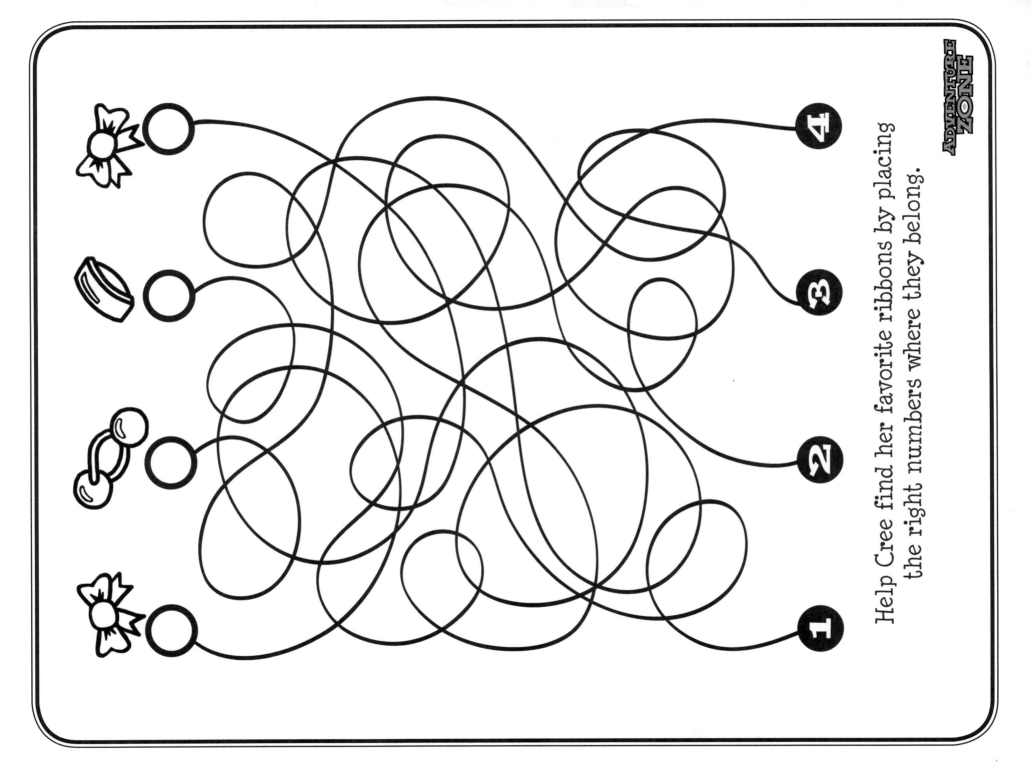

Help Cree find her favorite ribbons by placing the right numbers where they belong.

Cree and Scooter take an airplane to travel to British Columbia, Canada.

There are 11 things different between the two scenes. Can you find them?

Cree needs help skiing down the mountain.
Can you show her the way?

Canada's cold weather is making Scooter change colors. Can you guess which one?

FIND THE PROVINCES!

```
E A G K V Y B S C Q B F L S G N A S G M J R D C
Z Y B O R Z A E A N O N T A R I O I Z M R O Q T J
T M D O I M J L O S Z I T S I E Y N X M D C A U D
N X Z C T B C V D O K A I J G B D L Z A N A B M Z
Y S O X A J I S L A R V D T L W R N F B X P
S E S Z F S N S F G N U T Z D M D B Q J N K Z E X
W A Y C C D U A G M G X W C C C A O P X V Z M D Y
M Q T J S P X W N J E T R N D E K B F J R F Z U O
G I J N X J T U R R Z M N E H W G Q W U I X W S
A X H W P T I A O E V L A Y J F L A X N M L P W A
U N E O P J D P B D A D N Q U F S U N B H K N W I
L M H J C A F L H Q N W M C U B F E W Y K K Z P B
N I Q S Z C A U U A A I L G U B R U N X V B R J M
O D H X Q V M M L Q V T I M M S D L E W V Z L L U
T H T N J L Q D N W Q U A T E Z P V M N Q Y Q L
M X V G T M N U H S B Q Q P V C E H B F E S P N O
N G W Z J U A X E E M W E Q Z B A R E N G C C C
Q S D W O W U D S B H W S T L N X U E L V F V H
A Z K F M M N E E R E O O W K E N Q N G F Y A O S
E Q W L T J Y F U M C C M Z F J R Y S F Z Y W K I
T E C E F A I T M U L P C M T B L A W I T H J C T
N L I Y Q G B L A P U O H J F E T F I B U C B C I
B G V F U X K D D W B T S B W N O P C J B V Y U R
P R I N C E E D W A R D I S L A N D K K B T G X B
```

Alberta, British Columbia, Manitoba, New Brunswick, Newfoundland and Labrador, Nova Scotia, Ontario, Prince Edward Island, Quebec, and Saskatchewan.

Canada has 10 provinces. Can you help find them?

Cree finds a ski charm she wants to add to her
charm bracelet. She's so excited!

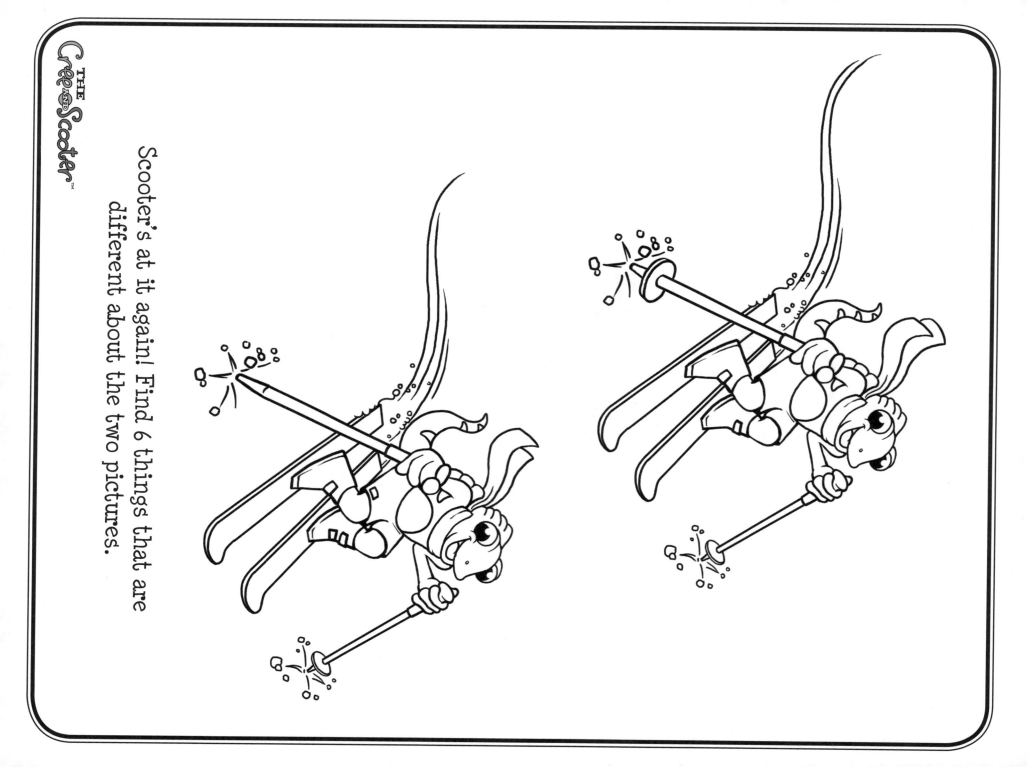

Scooter's at it again! Find 6 things that are different about the two pictures.

SCOOTER'S WORD FIND

BACKPACK
CANADA
MERCI
SKIING
CHAMELEON
OMAR
VANCOUVER
BRITISH COLUMBIA
CREE
SCOOTER
WHISTLER

B   G   R   X   C   C   S   N   I   C   A   N   A   D   A

K   R   L   E   T   E   L   K   U   M   Q   E   M   N   X

C   Z   I   U   L   G   M   S   I   H   X   P   E   J   M

F   E   N   T   V   T   Z   O   M   I   U   Z   R   H   K

D   V   I   T   I   A   S   B   C   V   N   K   C   F   D

X   Y   Z   X   V   S   I   A   J   U   G   I   E   C

R   W   B   O   N   O   H   N   H   R   Z   X   M   R   H

D   H   S   A   O   U   C   C   E   W   G   K   R   I   A

O   U   V   F   K   O   J   T   O   T   Y   T   Z   H   M

U   P   I   C   U   P   O   B   D   L   J   D   Q   C   E

J   J   M   V   T   O   P   U   Y   P   U   R   V   C   L

O   R   E   K   C   A   P   K   C   A   B   M   R   O   E

H   R   B   S   C   O   N   Y   H   N   J   E   B   O   O

B   O   S   V   H   B   R   A   M   O   E   F   R   I   N

W   J   L   W   B   S   B   I   A   A   P   O   Z   K   A

Scooter needs to find the missing words to
help him with his trip to Canada.
Circle each word you find.

TIC TAC TOE FUN!

SQUARE ME IN

Take turns connecting the dots. Write your initial inside every square you make. The one to form the most squares wins!

THE Creep AND Scooter™

CONNECT THE DOTS

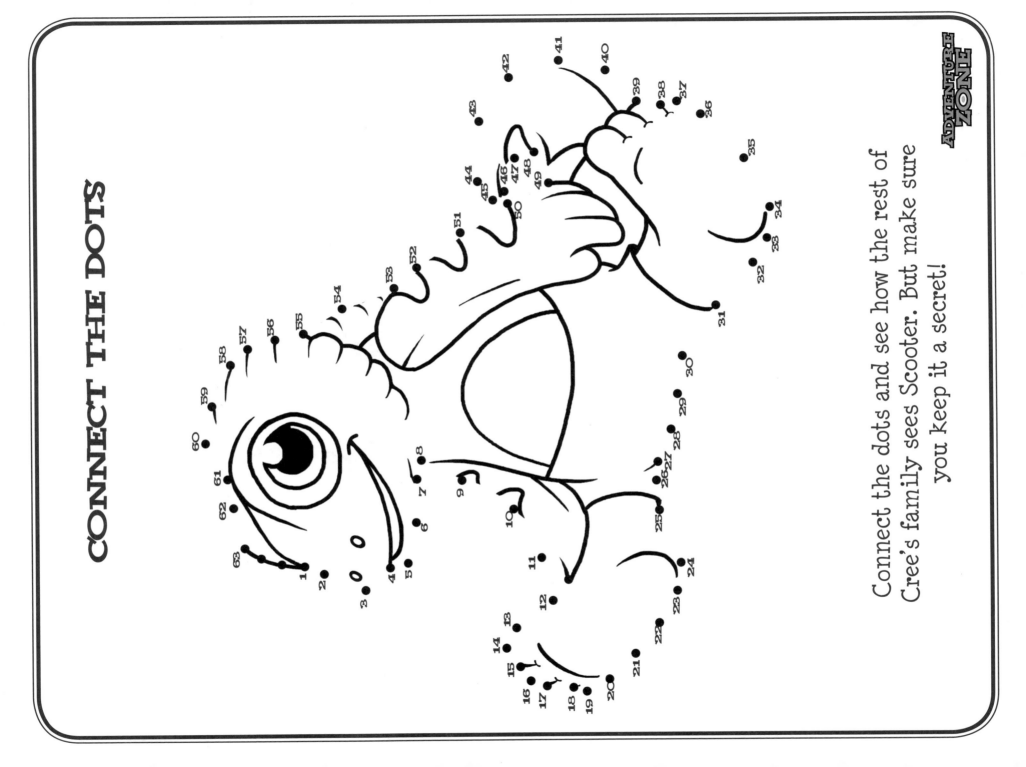

Connect the dots and see how the rest of Cree's family sees Scooter. But make sure you keep it a secret!

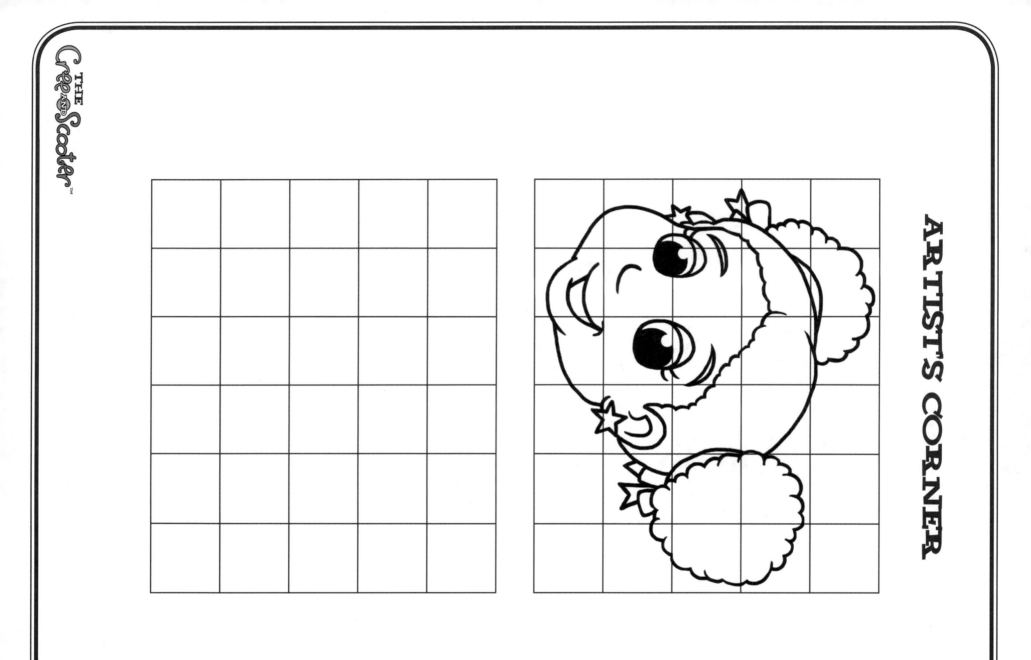

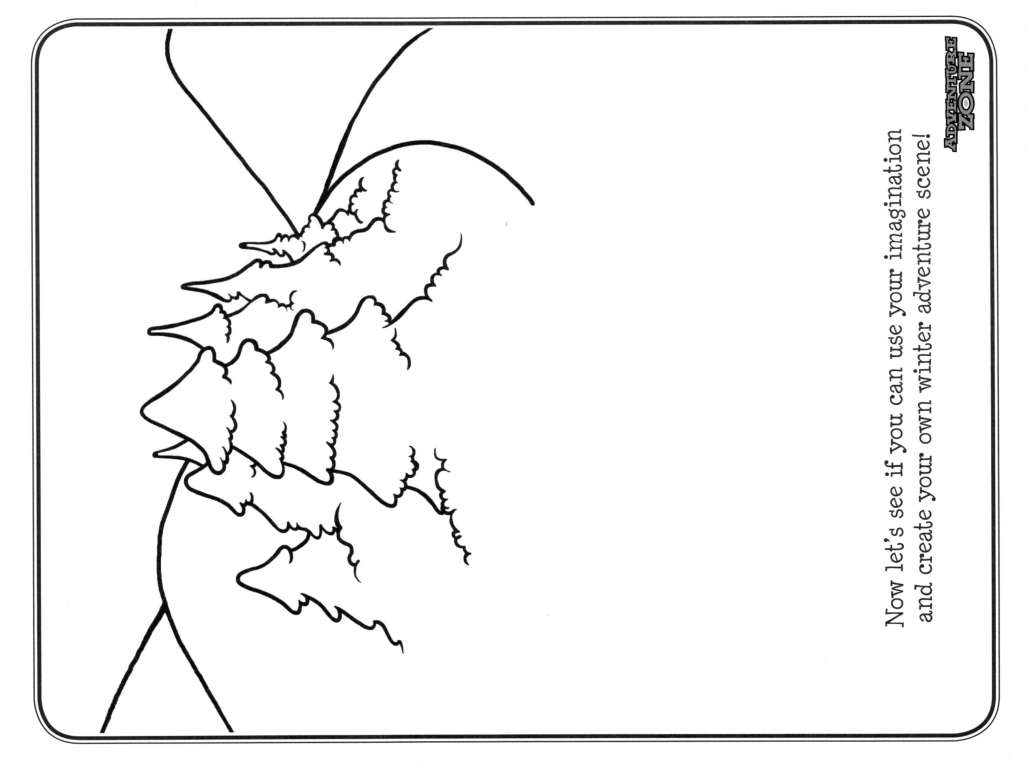

Now let's see if you can use your imagination
and create your own winter adventure scene!

PUZZLE ANSWERS

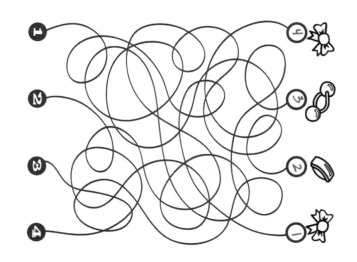

ONTARIO

PRINCEEDWARDISLAND

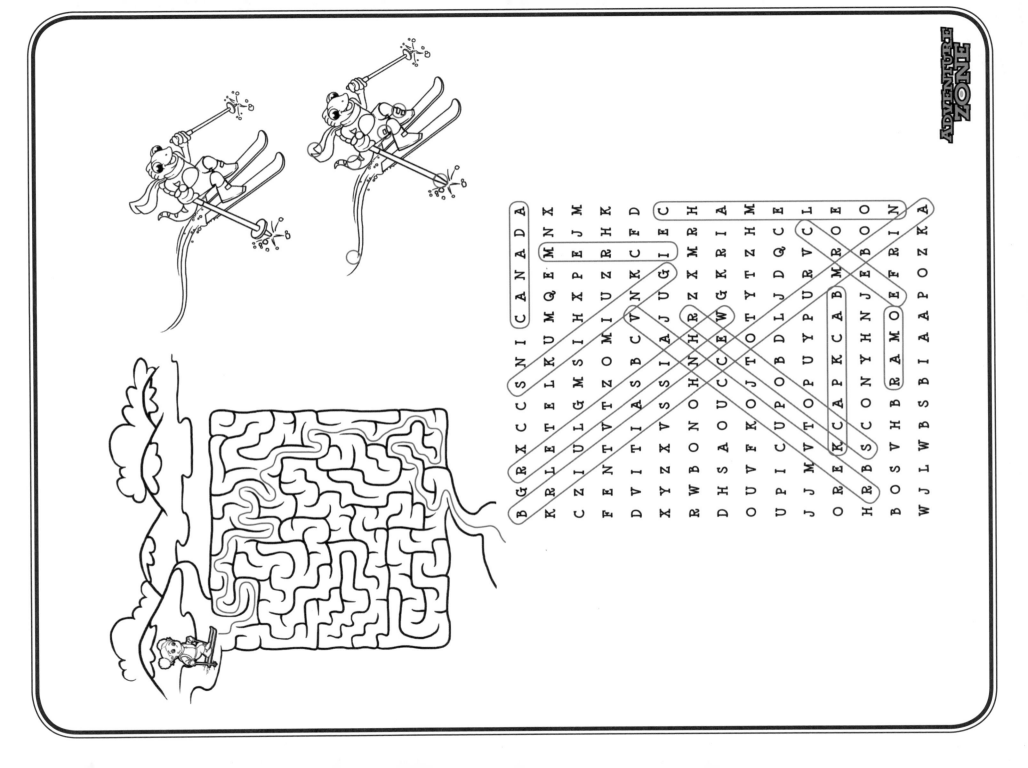